I'll Follow *the* Moon

I'll Follow the Moon

the Moon

Written *by* Stephanie Lisa Tara

Illustrated by Lee Edward Födi

10th Anniversary - Collector's Edition

Stephanie Lisa Tara
CHILDREN'S BOOKS

I'll Follow the Moon chronicles the journey of baby green sea turtles, nest to sea, exploring their extraordinary instinct to follow flickering moonlight home. Green sea turtle mothers deposit more than one hundred eggs in a subterranean beach nest, and after a two-month incubation period, the baby turtles hatch, dig to the surface, and crawl home to the sea.

© 2014 Stephanie Lisa Tara
Original illustrations by Lee Edward Fodi
Layout and design by Ted Ruybal
No toxic materials were used in the manufacturing of this book.

I'll Follow the Moon

Stephanie Lisa Tara Children's Books
1 Blackfield Drive Box #312
Tiburon, CA 94920

Preserve. Conserve. Inspire. Teach.

ISBN: 978-0-9894334-0-2
LCCN: 2011929050

Printed in the United States
10 9 8 7 6 5 4
Third Edition © 2013 Stephanie Lisa Tara/Lee Edward Fodi
Second Edition © 2008 Stephanie Lisa Tara/Lee Edward Fodi
First Edition © 2004 Stephanie Lisa Tara/Lee Edward Fodi

For more information about the author, or the book,
please visit: www.stephanielisatara.com.

Preserve. Conserve. Inspire. Teach.

Stephanie Lisa Tara
CHILDREN'S BOOKS

~For Aunt Barbara~
whose encouragement shines
as bright as the moon

Stephanie Lisa Tara discovered the power of verse at an early age. Her daughter Madeline is equally thrilled by it's wonderful whimsy and bouncing lyrical notes. A former ad copywriter, Stephanie truly appreciates the wit and wisdom of words. Having lived extensively on both US coasts and in western Europe, she is ever inspired by the universal language of storytelling and it's ability to teach and entertain children and parents alike. The Taras reside in beautiful northern California, living between redwood trees and the sea. Visit her web-site at www.StephanieLisaTara.com.

Lee Edward Födi has been writing and illustrating stories about all sorts of animals for as long as he can remember. Growing up on a farm, he was inspired by the company of countless creatures—hamsters, cats, dogs, parakeets, rabbits, frogs turtles, newts, and his very first pet: a blind and ruffled old hen. Many things have changed since his boyhood days, but Lee's love of nature has not. He currently lives and works on the west coast of Canada, where he enjoys an abundance of nature and the steady array of critters that frequent his neighborhood. Visit his web-site at www.leefodi.com.

What is it about turtles? Slow and steady, they win the race. In all ways. It's true, green sea turtles are endangered, and it's as if this little baby turtle knows it. He has championed his cause quietly, held the banner for ten years now, garnering awards and endorsements and praise—worldwide. What can we say about a one-inch little green-skinned infant like him? Well, we can honor him and his kind, as we honor all mothers everywhere. *I'll Follow the Moon*, written by a mom for all moms, is a tale of hope, love, and dreams. Yes, it's true that this little guy is tiny, but his heart is as big as the ocean, and will touch yours too.

One night in 2001, about a month after I brought baby Madeline home from the hospital, I noticed something quite strange on the beach in front of our south Florida home. It was late and Mom was tired. I was out on the deck, giving Maddie a last-one-of-the-day bottle feeding after a long day of new mom activities. As Maddie slurped down the final ounce of her formula with that familiar *glup, glup, glup* sound, I noticed dark, tiny shapes scurrying across the sand. *What is this?* I wondered, and I went down for a closer look. There they were: baby turtles streaming out of hundreds of small nests, with gentle rises in the sand as their markers. The babies made fanciful patterns in the sand as they dashed forward on their little green legs in a remarkable race to the sea. I watched them hop, one by one, into welcoming waves that sparkled under the beautiful moonlight. "I'm coming, Mama," they seemed to be saying, and I realized that I was witnessing one of nature's sacred events—the bond of love between mother and child. It was this precious feeling that inspired me to write *I'll Follow the Moon*, which came into being a few years later.

With love,
Stephanie Lisa Tara

Warm

Soft

Dry

I dream in blue.
Shimmering yellow,
And turquoise too.

I'm coming, Mama, I'll see you soon
I know just how . . . I'll follow the moon

Click

Clack

Tap

Blue melts away.
As I tap, crick, crack,
I spin, I sway.

I'm coming, Mama, I'll see you soon
I know just how . . . I'll follow the moon

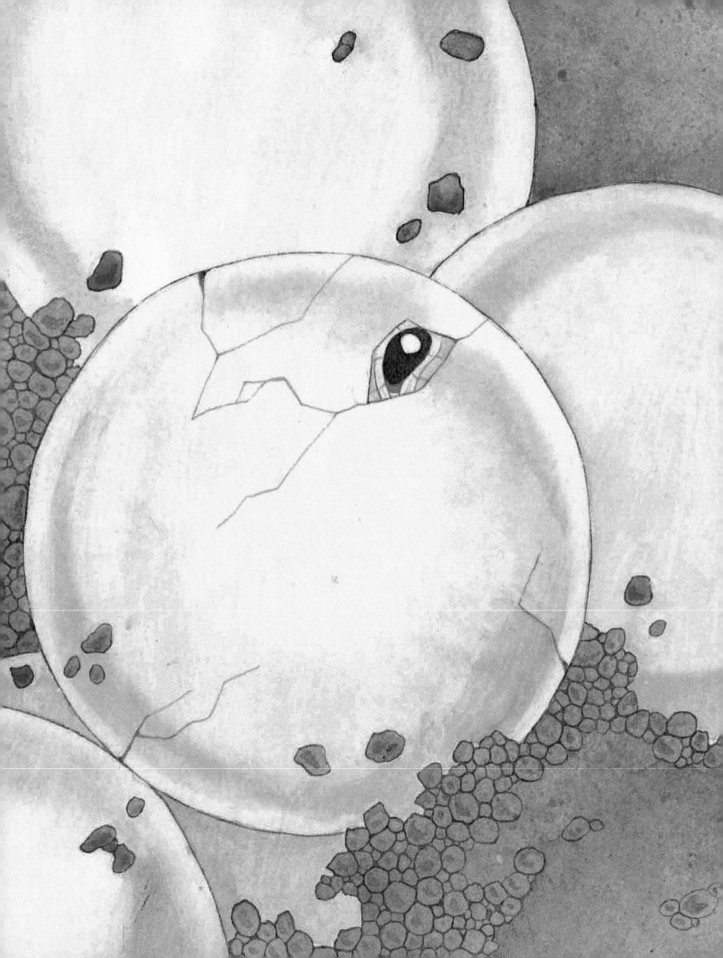

Roll
Slide
Tumble

I push, I shove.
Boom, bang, shake, and stop,
What is above?

I'm coming, Mama, I'll see you soon
I know just how . . . I'll follow the moon

Tap
Push
C r a c k

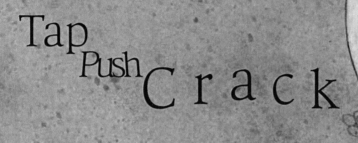

My beak breaks through.
A bit at a time,
All so new.

I'm coming, Mama, I'll see you soon

I know just how . . . I'll follow the moon

Out
Free
Lost

It's time to dig.
Through damp, sticky stuff,
Places so big.

I'm coming, Mama, I'll see you soon
I know just how . . . I'll follow the moon

Crawl
Scoop
Shove

My flippers glide.
From here, now to there,
They slip and slide.

I'm coming, Mama, I'll see you soon
I know just how . . . I'll follow the moon

Oops You Too

Why, we're the same.
With flippers flapping,
A special game.

I'm coming, Mama, I'll see you soon
I know just how . . . I'll follow the moon

Up   Around
   Down

Together, strong.
We each find a path,
It won't be long.

I'm coming, Mama, I'll see you soon
I know just how . . . I'll follow the moon

Whoosh
Night
Kiss

I breathe in deep.
Salt air on my face,
Turtle-heart leap!

I'm coming, Mama, I'll see you soon

I know just how . . . I'll follow the moon

Fine
Blue
Glow

Spill over me.
Oh moon, high above,
Eternity.

I'm coming, Mama, I'll see you soon
I know just how . . . I'll follow the moon

Stretch
Flex
Go

Under moon's sheen.
Stripes over my back,
Of deepest green.

I'm coming, Mama, I'll see you soon
I know just how . . . I'll follow the moon

Strong
Sure
Clear

Flippers move fast.
Moon sparkles my way,
Lights glitter past.

I'm coming, Mama, I'll see you soon
I know just how . . . I'll follow the moon

Wet
Spray
Tickle

Water on me.
Rushing, crashing sounds,
Much more to see.

I'm coming, Mama, I'll see you soon

I know just how . . . I'll follow the moon

Gulp

Spin

Float

I lose my place.
Water swirls me round,
Look for a face.

I'm coming, Mama, I'll see you soon
I know just how . . . I'll follow the moon

Swim
Look
Search

Moon knew the way.
Now here in my dream,
I wait, I stay.

I'm coming, Mama, I'll see you soon
I know just how . . . I'll follow the moon

Eyes
Like
Mine   Of deepest blue.
         Shell to shell we go,
         In love, anew.

I'm here Mama—here with you
I knew I'd find you, Moon did too.

Winner of the prestigious Chocolate Lily Award and the Mom's Choice Award, author **Stephanie Lisa Tara** and Canadian illustrator **Lee Edward Födi** have teamed up to create a lyrical rendition of a green sea turtle's first glimpse of life. Hatched on a moon-washed beach, the baby turtle finds it's way by instinct across the expanse of sand to the sea and a rendezvous with it's mother. Though science has only been able to prove that turtles seek the sea via moonlight, it is hard not to imagine they aren't seeking their mothers too.

Editorial Reviews

"This attractive book is an enjoyable way to introduce young listeners to a fascinating cycle in nature. Gorgeous watercolors chronicle the journey of a baby sea turtle from it's hatching to it's first swim in the sea."

—KIRKUS REVIEWS, September 2005

"Captivates children with poetry . . ."

—NEW YORK TIMES, December 2005

"Cleverly introduces young children to environmental awareness . . . young readers are educated so that they, and their parents, will become global citizens."

—SHARON STONE, Actress/Activist, January 2006

"All children want to have security, and they love animals. *I'll Follow the Moon* by Stephanie Lisa Tara is about both.

On a serene, quiet, sandy beach a baby sea turtle breaks free from it's egg and begins the journey to find home and mother, all the while saying, "I'm coming, Mama, I'll see you soon. I know just how . . . I'll follow the moon." And follow the moon to Mama is exactly what the baby sea turtle does. The simple words and gentle rhythm makes this a wonderful bedtime story. It is soothing and subtly conveys the message that Mother will be there for the child. The watercolor illustrations are solid, yet soft. They beautifully portray the beach and sky in an inviting way that adds to the soothing nature of the book.

Armchair Interviews says: Not only is this a wonderful story for parents to read to their little ones, but it is a book that grandparents will welcome as they care for their grandchildren. *I'll Follow the Moon* can help them assure their beloved grandchildren that their parents' absence is temporary. It is a lovely book that will be read and reread."

—ARMCHAIR INTERVIEWS, December 2005

"In this tranquil bedtime story, a baby sea turtle hatches on the beach and wants to find his mother. And he knows just how—he'll follow the moon! From his gentle struggles to break free of his egg to his determination to dig his way out of the sand nest and his eager shuffles toward the ocean, we follow the baby sea turtle on each step of his instinctive journey back to his loving mother who awaits him to the sea. Stephanie Lisa Tara's gentle verse, along with Lee Edward Födi's soft, earth-toned illustrations, capture the gentle and natural beauty of this nocturnal beach migration. Your young readers and listeners will be rooting for the young sea turtle as he works his way toward the sea and thrilled to see him reunite with his mother, even as they discover the beauty of this real life struggle of the green sea turtle."

—BOOKS OF WONDER
Peter Glassman, December 2007

Click, clack, tap,
Blue melts away. As I tap, crick, crack, I spin, I sway.
I'm coming Mama, I'll see you soon
I know just how . . . I'll follow the moon.

"Written in simple verse in the first person, the rhythmic text is full of action and sensory detail and loaded with alliteration and onomatopoeia for an enjoyable read-aloud. The atmosphere of a quiet but determined struggle to break free of the egg soon gives way to growing excitement as the turtle mingles with fellow hatchlings and catches his first tempting sensations: the smell of salt air, the sight of the moon's glow, the gentle touch and beckoning sounds of the waves rushing to shore. Once he's free of the land, new motions take over: gulp, spin, float, swim. . . . The final happy refrain is new and satisfying: "I'm here, Mama—here with you. I know I'd find you, Moon did too." Framed by end-papers of soft, limitless, undersea green, Fodi's delightful illustrations feature an animated and engaging baby emerging from an egg buried in golden sand. With other tiny turtles, he is shown plowing through the damp sand, sampling the salty sea air, and marching unerringly toward the moonlight glimmer, his guide to the ocean. Once afloat, he soon comes face to face with 'eyes like mine' in his new watery home. The gold of sand, blue of sky, and green of the sea repeated throughout the book bring a sense of harmony. The turtle is the focal point of all the pictures, with few background details added. The illustrator has carefully integrated the turtle's actions with Tara's verse, which relies heavily on verbs: roll, slide, tumble, crawl, scoop, shove. Young children will be propelled through the story in the illustrations as well as the text."

—CANADIAN MATERIALS MAGAZINE
Gillian Richardson, September 2005. Highly Recommended.

Customer Reviews

MY DAUGHTER LOVED IT!:

"My daughter loved the turtle. The illustrations are great! She said,
"Mom if I'm ever lost, I'll follow the moon and find you.""

MY PRESCHOOLER LOVES THIS BOOK:

"My 3 1/2 year old daughter loves this book. She has learned the little saying that is on every page
and loves to say it with me."

GENTLE REPETITION:

"The story is gentle and the repetition helps soothe my son. I like the message, and the art is beautiful."

GREAT BOOK:

"Great book for the grandkids. They love it. They like to read prior to bedtime.
The girls really enjoy this book."

I'LL FOLLOW THE MOON:

"This children's book has beautiful illustrations that compliment the lyrical, gentle words that accompany
the small sea turtle's journey from egg to sea."

SO CUTE!:

"It's impossible not to be enchanted by these little creatures! I'm so in love with this book,
perfect for everyone!"

CUTE BEDTIME STORY:

"I enjoyed reading this book to my daughter, she loved the artwork.
It was well written and will be enjoyable for children."

BEAUTIFUL ILLUSTRATIONS:

"What a lovely book! A great story to introduce an environmental concept."

WONDERFUL STORY:

"I can't say enough about the wonderful story in this book. If I child loves the moon, it's perfect. If a child loves
turtles, it's perfect. The perfect book to read to a child of any age."

I'LL FOLLOW THE MOON:

"I really enjoyed this book. I read it to my 1 and 2 year old. They really enjoyed this book.
Beautiful illustration!"

FANTASTIC:

"A perfect afternoon read. I enjoyed it, and my son will too I'm sure."

SWEET AND PERTINENT:

"As a resident of northwest Florida, this book is one that should be shared with all residents, young and old alike. It is currently turtle season here and all residents enjoy keeping watch on these special creatures."

SWEET CHILDREN'S BOOK:

"A sweet children's book, lovely rhymes and beautiful pictures. Definitely a book worth having to enjoy over and over, great for kids of any age."

GREAT TO READ ALOUD TO THE CLASS:

"My second graders will love this simple book with wonderful words and a repetitive line which they will quickly join in to read."

I'LL FOLLOW THE MOON:

"I read this to my boys. They loved the graphics and how cute the turtles were. The story is super cute! Very entertaining."

SWEET SIMPLE STORY, SWEET ILLUSTRATIONS:

". . . comforting and relaxing. The story line is not at all complex, but is appealing in its simplicity and repetitiveness."

MAKES A GREAT BEDTIME STORY!:

". . . decided to download it for my kid's...Cute illustrations, educational, and delivers a positive message. Makes a great bedtime story. Recommend it!"

LOVED IT:

"Sweet sweet book! Repetitive so I think it's great for children to be able to read along. Educational as well. A must have for a sea turtle lover! The illustrations were great!"

WE LOVE THIS STUDY!:

"My kids love this story, we read it in the evenings and they enjoy it over and over! Illustrations are beautiful! Enjoy this beautiful book!"

LOVELY STORY TO READ WITH YOUR CHILDREN:

". . . I am always looking for books that teach a bit in the midst of their story lines . . . meaningful to children of all ages . . . truly a story you and your children will treasure."

VERY CUTE!:

"Wonderful book, very interesting, beautiful story with illustrations. Teaching my daughters to love and care for turtles just like I do!"

A CHILDHOOD FAVORITE:

"Delightfully written is the story of a young sea turtle making his first trip to the sea. The artwork is beautiful and the introduction to the endangered turtles to children is perfect."

WONDERFUL BOOK:

"This is the most wonderful little book. My children will be happy to each own a copy for them to keep at Christmas. I wish that you will keep writing and illustration these marvelous books. Anxious to see your next one."

ONE HAPPY MOMMA!:

"What an amazingly well written kids book! My two boys love it! My 8 year old son loves reading it to our 4 month old. Thank you Stephanie Lisa Tara!"

GREAT BEDTIME STORY!:

"Wonderful illustrations and bedtime story. Great for kids and teaching them about sea turtles and nature. Great price for such a nice book!!"

SPLENDID!:

"This publication is worth sharing, as a gift or for your children. Especially for Turtle enthusiasts. My children love it:)"

I'LL FOLLOW THE MOON:

"I'll follow the Moon is a heartwarming book that shows how strong the bond is between a mother and her child. My son loves sea turtles and this book is one of his favorite books to read."

WONDERFUL FOR ALL AGES:

"I work at a daycare / pre-school, and have this book set into my lesson plans every year!! The children love it every year!"

THE ABSOLUTE BEST CHILDREN'S BOOK I HAVE READ IN YEARS!:

"This book is perfection, from the illustrations to the story. I bought one for my niece, and I actually have one for myself. (Always loved turtles) it's a good tale of hope, and positivity. All my nieces and nephews will be getting a copy!"

COMPLETELY DELIGHTFUL!!!!!!!:

"I absolutely adore this book. I am not sure which I like more, the story itself or the beautiful illustrations!!!!"

LOVE THIS BOOK:

"My son is absolutely OBSESSED with turtles, especially Sea Turtles. I downloaded this book on my kindle and he read it right away. Absolutely LOVES it. And he asks to read it daily!! Thank you for writing such a great book!!"

BEAUTIFUL BOOK!:

"I read this to my son every night before bead. The rhyming verses, repetition and beautiful illustrations are peaceful and calming before bed. This is by far one of my favorite books for children."

LOVE!!:

"My 2 year old loves this book!! Whenever I tell her to get a book for story time,

this is the one she grabs!!"

GREAT BOOK!:

"After reading this novel to my youngest brother, I couldn't help but read it again. I am a huge lover of turtles and this book helped replenish that love. I found it informative but also adorable. With a title like that, how else could you not pick up this book. I recommend it to all readers out there if you have a young sibling, young son/daughter, or if you're bored and want to read a great book about turtles. Again, fantastic book and I hope I can read more!!"

SUCH A CUTE CHILDREN'S BOOK!:

"I love love love this book! It very cutely and accurately describes this little turtle's journey from hatching on! After doing volunteer work with the Hawaii Island Hawksbills as well as working closely with the Greens, I can't help seem to stop myself from buying every turtle related book I find!"

GREAT BOOK!!!! A MUST HAVE!!!!:

"Wow . . . this book is sooo enchanting my little girl loved it, I would totally recommend it for all children, girls and boys! The pictures are awesome and the story kept my daughter interested and engaged to the end!!!"

AWESOME BOOK:

"I loved this book! I love sea turtles, and I love books but I haven't found a sea turtle book that I have really loved until this one! I'm glad I read it and everyone children and adults should have this!!!"

WONDERFUL CHILDREN'S BOOK:

"I have been working in sea turtle conservation for a number of years so of course we had to get this book for our young granddaughters. They love it! When they actually got to see baby turtles last summer they remembered the facts they learned in this book. I highly recommend it."

ONE OF THE BEST:

"This is one of the best children's books I have read in a long time. I love the illustrations and the story line. A must read for you and your children!"

GREAT STORY FOR YOUNG KIDS:

"My 19.5mo old son brings me this book Daily saying "Momma Tuttle, please Tuttle." He loves Turtles & loves to mimic me while reading this book. It's so cute and we love the drawings. He also just realized what the moon was outside so when he sees it in the book he associates it with outside. This really is a great book for young children and I'm sure older kids as well."

IT'S SO CUTE!:

"I love it! I love turtles, and the story is great! I read it every night after I have a hard day and it makes me feel a lot better! Thank you to my Grandma who got me this book! I love you Grandma!"

A WONDERFUL, EDUCATIONAL BOOK FOR CHILDREN!:

"A wonderful children's book that is very educational and has wonderful pictures! Makes a great bedtime story and is highly recommended!"

I'LL FOLLOW THE MOON:

"A wonderful gentle story that can teach your little one about the amazing sea turtles! The illustrations were lovely."

*All above published reviews can be found at I'LL FOLLOW THE MOON'S Amazon page.

I'LL FOLLOW THE MOON:

"I stumbled across this book quite by accident, and I found it to be a treasure. The verse is lovely and calm, as are the illustrations. It also depicts fairly accurately a remarkable natural phenomenon. As a new mom who longed for a child for many years and eventually adopted internationally, I found the symbolism achingly beautiful. I have since given the book to several friends who have also waited for their children to find them. This book is far too beautiful to be limited to the adoption genre, however. It is very meaningful on a number of different levels!"

WONDERFUL BOOK FOR LITTLE TURTLE LOVERS:

"I got this for my daughter, who loves turtles, and it did not disappoint. Lovely illustrations paired with a sweet story of the life of a sea turtle hatching making its way in the world made it an instant hit for all our children."

SWEET, POETIC BOOK:

"My daughters (4 and 2) are going through a big turtle phase which is why I got this. The story is very sweet and reassuring to a child (spoiler alert: the baby turtle DOES find mommy and they are reunited with much joy). The poetic writing and gorgeous illustrations—and heavy, sturdy paper—makes this a nice aesthetic experience for the adult reading aloud, also."

ENCHANTING LITTLE TURTLE:

"As a mother, Middle School Language Arts teacher, and earlier as an elementary school teacher and reading teacher specialist, I would have given anything for a book as well written and inspiring as "I'll Follow the Moon." Stephanie Lisa Tara is obviously a gentle creature herself who realizes the connections between all of nature. In a divine act that most of us would find merely delightfully scientific, she found the invisible thread of the maternal bond. Moreover, her repeating verse is genius. Children learn from repetition, and repeating verse is the surest style for reinforcing sight words, developing an ear for inflexion, gaining understanding of fluency, and building reading confidence. Her sweet verse sounds like the cry of a child's heart that all children are sure to identify with and the descriptive words and phrases woven in between the verse challenge the mind of the reader and older children as well while creating inspiration for conversation. This book is rife with learning potential and pure joy. I love reading it to my little granddaughter, who is nearly four now. She anticipates the verse and joins it. She is inspired to question the meaning of all kinds of things as we read it, and I am pressed to keep the tears of pride that well in my eyes from spilling over each time. I appreciate that she is learning pre-reading skills and is being introduced to the sea turtle, part of her heritage and ecological responsibilities as a native North Carolinian. I also love all the amazing thoughts it provokes in her for us to discuss, some new question or thought on her part each time. Thank you, Ms. Tara, you took a simple act of nature and opened all our eyes. Your pure hearted spirit shines in this priceless and multifaceted literary enchantment."

I LOVE THIS BOOK:

"I just picked this up for my daughter's 3rd birthday and I think I like it more than she does. It reads like a song and the illustrations are very sweet and happy. Great bedtime story."

GREAT STORY:

"This story is beautifully illustrated and the concept is amazing. We loved it! My son enjoyed the art work and I enjoyed reading it to him."

A TRUE CLASSIC . . . PERFECT GIFT!:

"This is a beautiful story and the illustrations are superb! I've given this as a gift . . . always a big hit!"

CHARMINGLY POETIC AND BEAUTIFULLY ILLUSTRATED:

"Charmingly poetic and beautifully illustrated . . . this sweet tale of a baby turtle hatching and finding his way to the sea and his mother is a wonderful example to little ones of the joys and peace of nature and the life cycle. The gorgeous soft earth tones of the drawings perfectly accompany the sweet story. I loved the rhyming verses and the repetition:

I'm coming, Mama, I'll see you soon

I know just how . . . I'll follow the moon

Is perfect for captivating and drawing in the participation of small children. It's engaging and beautiful, calming and inspiring . . . everything that one would hope for in a children's book. Don't hesitate to pick up this book for your little one or as a gift if you want to share a wonderful message about the beauty and hope of Mother Nature." Great book and gift!

"This has been one of our "go to" books for birthdays as it seems that everyone always gives the same standard books. The children have all loved it!! It is a great bedtime or anytime story."

I'LL FOLLOW THE MOON:

"Thanks to Stephanie Lisa Tara's I'll Follow The Moon and the Turtle Book I am now in love with sea turtles. I'll Follow The Moon is a very sweet story about a baby sea turtle hatching and following the moon to get into the water to find his mama. The pictures are so cute. I recommend this children's book if you like sea turtles but even if you don't you might end up liking sea turtles after reading this book and also Stephanie Lisa Tara's Turtle Book."

ONE OF THE BEST . . . !:

"This is one of the best children's books I have ever read! My son, who loves turtles, is inspired to read with this book. Stephanie Lisa brilliantly incorporates the adventure of a baby sea turtle hatching from his egg to his trip into the sea, all the while following the moon to find his mother. The illustrations are beautiful. A must read!"

SUPERB ARTWORK:

"Award winning illustrations and a subject matter for me that is dear to my heart! One book I will be passing onto some friends of ours as well whose daughter is very active with sea turtles having worked with them in Florida, Nicaragua and Australia. Very good children's book!"

KUDOS:

"My granddaughter Kawehi enjoyed this very much . . . she was able to understand and follow the story line . . . . No wonder they got so many deserving accolades!"

EXCELLENT BOOK FOR YOUNG AND OLD ALIKE:

"Both young and old can enjoy this excellent book of following your heart and your dreams. Teaches us all to keep dreaming!"

WORKS EVERY TIME TO PUT MY DAUGHTER TO SLEEP:

"This is a wonderful book that my daughter has been requesting every night and before I finish she is fast asleep. Thank you!"

*All above published reviews can be found at I'LL FOLLOW THE MOON'S Amazon page.

Made in the USA
Middletown, DE
19 June 2015